WRITTEN BY:
KEITH BLAIR
AKA
ANTHONY B

Copyright © 2019 by Keith Blair aka Anthony B

All rights reserved. This book or any portion thereof may not be reproduced or used in any manner whatsoever without the express written permission of the publisher except for the use of brief quotations in a book review.

First edition April 2019

Author: Keith Blair aka Anthony B
Cover by: João Albuquerque
Composition: António Santos,
in characters, Literata Book, body 10

http://www.officialanthonyb.com/

Table of Contents

Introduction	1
STEP 1: Erase your doubts	3
STEP 2: Face your fears	9
STEP 3: Admit you care	19
STEP 4: Full attention	25
STEP 5: Overcome temptations	35
STEP 6: Have strong faith	43
STEP 7: The commitment	53
The way to the key	63

·Introduction·

On a snowy afternoon

a sudden leap of faith

turns up as the answer

to a long and ongoing debate in my mind about self-love and the blanket of self-hate.

"Can a man truthfully, honestly, openly, or secretly, stay faithfully in love looking at all the temptations of the world?", I ask myself.

Is it so hard for a man

to truly choose one partner above all others?

Yes, I am a man. Lies are not new to me. Swearing and saying I'm sorry for all the wrongs that I have done and for all that I have put you through. And also for what I am about to do now.

Men will be men and that's what men do.

Here it goes again. All in to me. Never thinking of you.

The art of love and acceptance

has opened my eyes to the essence

and the full meaning of how two hearts exist as one.

STEP

· Erase your doubts ·

STEP

· *Erase your doubts* ·

I was at a tender age, the first time I got this feeling deep inside of my belly sitting there in my class room one day, when I saw this beautiful girl walk in.

I could tell it was her first day at school, because I had never seen her before. Suddenly, my heart stopped. It was like nothing I had experienced before.

In the little town where I grew up, if I had a girl looking like this girl is looking right now. Wow, all the people would be calling her an angel and me a king!

Yes, I had a lot of childhood girlfriends in school and in the community I call home. We would play around and write love letters saying all kinds of things about love and making all kinds of promises.

Still I never had this feeling before that I was feeling right now sitting here looking at this beautiful new girl as she slowly passed by me to take her seat.

All the kids in the classroom turned their heads, not to mention the boys! By lunchtime, they started a betting match.

That afternoon when all the other kids were on the playground having fun, the only thing on my mind was how beautiful and attractive this new girl in class was. I started wondering away deeper in my thinking pattern, "What would it take to gain her attention and win her love?"

It took three weeks to gather the courage to make the first step, to try and utter my first word to her.

As I got closer, the feeling was more like a heart attack. Instantly my breathing stopped, and I started to wonder to myself, "What's wrong with me?"

I wanted to talk to her, but I never could find the words to say.

***

Commitment is like a lily. It needs water to show its glory. Can a man be faithful?

There are so many ways to find love: twitter, facebook, online, bbm, ig, various dating services... and the list goes on. Looking for love.

Is that love? Hell, yea it is.

Growing up on the streets taught us to love no one, trust no one. Macho, gangsta thug life, bad man. That's all I knew.

For a man to drop his arms is like taking his self-esteem away.

I see love like it's just a word that people say a lot. It's much easier to say than for people to express what their hearts are truly feeling.

When I lie to my friends, they feel better about themselves. But are they really better in themselves?

So this life becomes our reality. I learn to face my problems with a fighting plan. The learning ways are too slow for me.

STEP

· Face your fears ·

STEP

· Face your fears ·

Having two or three girls that make a man feel like king Solomon.

Or sharing power with a woman?

No woman can rule me. Women like to control and take over a man's life. Your life is over the moment you fall in love.

Can a woman truly love? When it's much quicker for a woman to be chased after than a man? She can have another me in a minute.

They are so emotional and always ask a lot of questions. They dig too deep sometimes.

That's what they call a woman's intuition.

I'm too tough for this love thing. It will surely cramp my style.

Men can't take a lot of stress or attention. It's a mental state we call "manhood."

Looking at my friends in love, falling in and out of love, getting kids, making a family, getting married and divorced.

I watch kids grow up like me on the streets, not by choice, just a product of a broken home. Where to go? What will they become?

Mom and dad fall out of love, so they move apart from each other. Daddy is off to the next city. Mommy is getting married again so she will move to London to live with her new husband.

I swear I will never fall in love, I'm just going to live my life single and free of love.

***

I have been saying all these things to myself, thinking it will make my life better, when I am so lonely deep down inside, hiding behind my fears and running away from all who seem to care.

Finally, I was swept away that snowy afternoon driving home from the airport.

Just arrived from a long flight coming from Paris, where I was out clubbing and masquerading, drinking, dancing to the music and the amazing night life of France all weekend.

Thankful for my return and all the fun I had, you could

see it on my face if I was committed. There was no way I could have let it stay hidden. I say to myself, "I'm so happy I am single. What a life! Wow!"

My business and my career granted me the privilege to travel a lot and so I got to see a lot of the world and experience many different cultures.

"I'm so happy with my way of life." I think to myself, my ego taking over my mind.

I got to the parking lot, got in my car. As I entered and got my car started, on the radio was a song my mom used to play when I was younger called Take time to know her. I smiled to myself as I drove out.

Outside was 30 degrees. So much snow was falling on the windshield of the car, the wiper could not hold it anymore.

I turned up the heater in an attempt to clear the windshield. It did not help. The road just kept getting more impossible to drive on.

Pulling over was not an option since there was no soft shoulder, just a narrow windy road! No chains on my tyres. I see trucks sliding off the road!

This is getting way too dangerous for me to keep driving. There is no road in front of me anymore. It's all white, looking like a milky river, there is no way to see the road signs. Nothing!

The only thing on my mind at this time was, "How will I get out of this?" I was praying so hard. The situation was getting worse by the minute. I tried calling 911. That's when I realized the cell phone had no service.

The wind kept getting stronger and the snow started falling harder than before. Now it was looking more like around 9 to 12 inches of snow on the road.

I could hear a rumbling sound like thunder and the drops from the snow falling on the roof of the car. Right now it was looking more like a big storm coming this way. I could see that there was a building coming down from faraway.

I was trying to get a better view out of the snowy window. I was starting to get disarrayed by uncertainty. What was this sound I was hearing?

Suddenly, something hit my car. The car started rolling over and over.

***

It took the paramedics a great deal of time to get me out. They used tools to cut through the door of the car.

I could see flashing lights from the numerous emergency vehicles surrounding my car, working very hard to get me out.

I could hear a voice asking me, "Are you ok, sir? Stay still, we are doing our best to get you out."

The voice sounded to me like a voice from out of this world, so soft-spoken and gentle, like an angel talking to me.

I started to wonder again and kept looking at myself to make sure I was still alive.

Then the door came flying off into the air. They finally did it. They cut me out.

I climbed out, and the doctor took me by my hands. He said, "Lie on this bed." I tried to tell him I was ok, but they had to do some mandatory tests to make sure I was ok before I could go home.

I was now in the ambulance on my way to the nearest hospital. They were taking me to meet the head doctor.

The room door swung open and this beautiful smiling doctor walked in. As she approached me closer, with each step she took, I felt the same feeling I had as a teenage boy.

It was a feeling of numbness and lost breath. She said to the nurse, "Is this the patient who was in the accident?"

The nurse quickly replied, "Yes, doctor."

STEP

· Admit you care ·

STEP

· *Admit you care* ·

She turned to me and asked, "What's your name, sir?" I could not speak. I was once again, at a loss for words.

"Can a man really fall in love?"

The question still lingered in my mind.

I found the words and replied, "Yes, doctor, my name I…" I stopped for a moment and smiled, then went on, "I want to know what love is."

She then said to me in a soft tone, "I am your doctor, and I don't talk to my patients like that."

I said to her, "After you check on me and I am much better to leave the hospital, I won't be your patient then. I will wait."

She replied, "You will wait on me now, and then after, what will you be expecting to happen?"

I replied, "We can talk and get to know each other."

She said, "Can we? No, I don't think so." She stopped for a second and looked at me. "Why are you acting like you don't know me from a long time ago? Try to remember. We are from the same hometown. We attended the same school and also we were in the same classroom. You haven't said a word to me in school, so why now?"

"Oh my god, it's your pretty smile!" I replied, "I just never got the guts to step up to you when we were in school. I tried many times just to find the courage to express myself and my true feelings to you.

I have lived a lifetime from those days, hoping I would see you again and you are not married, and I find the confidence to make my moves to let you know what's in my heart all these years.

The real truth is, you give me a weakness deep in my belly every time I am in your presence."

She smiled but said nothing. She then went on to check me and told me I was good. "No bones broken and no serious damage has been done by the accident. You are a lucky man."

In the back on my mind I am saying, "I am really a lucky man." This is what it took to get my first moment with someone I had been dreaming of for so long.

I then went ahead one more time and asked for her number. She gave me her number and said, "We will talk. A little talk never hurts."

"Yes, yes," I say to myself. I was so excited.

Anyway, I kept that thought to myself and said, "Thanks a lot for your magical hands and willingness to serve. I hope to keep our contact strong, I just want you to know, there is no me or you in love. It's just us."

In the back of my mind, though, I'm thinking, "Don't we all say that to ourselves?"

I am not a man of many words, but at this moment I just could not get up and go without expressing myself in a humble way, so I said, "When I was in the car rolling over, I asked myself these questions:

'What is the value of life?'

'What is it worth living for? And what is it worth dying for?'

'What is the mark I want to make on this world?'

'And what are the memories I want to leave in my legacy? '

When you live a single life, what happens when you need someone's helping hands, touch, words, or just some emotional support? I'm here looking in your eyes now, and I can see the answers to all my question is the same one: love.

Now I plan to walk with dignity and live up to the truth.

I never knew in my lifetime I would be needing someone to share my life with. I can surely tell you right here, right now, my lying days are over and my days of being a cheater and a player have come full circle.

I see now the true meaning of life. I don't want to wait on that day to come when I truly need someone's hands or voice to say, 'Are you ok?'"

She listened quietly and then said, "Call me tomorrow, if you are not just a sweet talker."

***

I left the hospital, stepped into the street and yelled for a cab. One pulled over and I got in it.

It felt so good being inside a warm cab. I said good night to the cab driver and he said, "Good night, sir. How is the weather treating you man?"

I replied, "It's all good. I just got out of a near-death accident. I have so much to give thanks for."

"It's a lesson well learned," he replied. "You must give thanks every day, all day. There is so much going on in the world today. Life is great. It's good to be alive."

I said, "Yes, that's for real." Then the cab driver turned his radio on. Here goes the next love talk.

The art of love: Can a man be faithful and truthful? Not lie anymore?

Psychologist Abraham Maslow wrote The Hierarchy of Human Needs. He said that the need for security is so fundamental to human development that we can't fulfill any other part of our potential until it is satisfied. To give and to receive love, he said, we must first trust our surroundings.

The cab stopped at a stop light and the cab driver turned to me and said, "That was deep," and then asked, "Are you married?"

I replied, "No, I'm not."

He said, "I got married 25 years ago."

I said, "That's great, and congrats for being married for a very long time."

He said, "Sir, when you get a good one, hold on to her. There are a lot of women out there, but not everything that shines is a gold coin. Some are just light to blind you from your real self and destroy the true meaning of love. It's so sad how men treat women in these days."

I said, "It's true. Anyway, I am stopping here. Thanks for your time and the advice. Have a safe night."

STEP

· Full attention ·

STEP

Full attention

I stepped out the cab and walked towards my house. What the cab driver was talking about was hitting me hard in my heart.

I don't think a man should have one woman. It's a free world.

Now something started to happen to my style and my way of thinking. Why was there doubt in my mind. Was this a good feeling or a bad one?

I was inside at last, and it felt good to be home. I had been through a lot. I decided to have a shower and head to bed.

The phone rang. It was one of my thug friends checking if I was in town and wondering how my trip was. I replied, "Great. We will talk tomorrow. I had a rough day."

He said "Alright, talk tomorrow," and hung up the phone.

I could not wait for daybreak. First thing in the morning I called my doctor. She answered the phone and said, "Hello. What's up?"

I replied, "What's up, my love?"

She said, "I am your love already?"

I said, "From the day you were born, you're my gift from god."

She laughed and said, "Your mouth is sweet like honey."

I said, "And so is my love."

She said, "You move fast."

"No time to waste," I replied. "I have been doing that all my life. Now is my time to know what love is. Come on, teacher, teach me everything I want to learn."

She said, "Sure you want to learn? I never hear that from a man…that he wants to learn."

I said to her, "That's why we keep on failing tests of love. If we don't take the time out as a man to learn from a woman what makes her happy, how can we make her happy? It's good to be loved by someone."

Then she replied, "Wait, are you for real? No man has ever talked to me like that."

I said, "I know, it's so bad for us as men." I never gave her the time to say another word before I asked her, "What's your plan for later? Can we go out and have a drink?"

I could only hear her say, "Too fast. You're gonna learn

from me now what's worth having and worth working for. That's gonna be your first lesson."

I then replied patiently, "That's okay. Thanks for your time and we will talk soon." I got off the phone.

I used to see this like a regret. But now I can see that talking to someone about love doesn't always go as planned and there is nothing wrong with that.

The problem is the f-word (fear).

When fear builds up in your safety center, the heart constricts, and often we end up in the wrong relationship. Sometimes the fear of getting hurt causes us to cut ourselves off from people around us. If we let fear dominate us and don't feel an inner sense of safety anymore, we will lose touch with love.

Is there a meaning to love?

There are no words to explain.

Here I am now. My mind cloudy, and in a wonder state. Asking myself, "Where do I go from here? Can I go through this? Is this what I really want?

Can I do this? Is it that hard just to have someone to care for you or just to reason with? Is this too much for a man to handle?

Is it that bad when your lady always wants to show you how much she is thinking of you? I want to be the only man for my woman, so I guess that's all she is asking of me."

What do you think?

Out of the blue, my doorbell rang. I shouted out in a loud voice, "Who is it?"

Someone replied. It was a man. I recognized the voice and went to open the door. It was one of my thug friends. He shouted to me, "What's up, mi doops? Are you ok? I heard about the road accident yesterday."

I said, "Out of every bad comes a good."

He asked, "What do you mean? What happened?"

I said, "I met someone. I think I am in love with her."

He replied, "You get lick up, love? No love no deh again, you just enjoy life and live. All a woman wants is man, money and time."

I replied, "You think giving in to only one woman in these times, my thug, is wrong? I know there are many girls out there. They say there are 21 women for each man. That's what statistics say. But you don't think there is someone special for everyone? Like a soulmate? That one love that makes you feel like you want to surrender it all to one person?"

He turned and said, "My thug, a lose you a lose it, one girl kill man nature, man fi have a new girl every night, you done know say dem girl yah now out a street cold like ice."

I replied, "We are done talking. Some lessons in life can't be taught. We have to live and experience them for ourselves, and then we will learn from them. I think I have been there and done that.

Can a boy be a boy forever? He has to one day realize he is grown, so he has to stand up and be a man. A man is not scared for someone to have their best interest in their heart."

He said, "Ok, my thug, I will see what comes out of this love you are talking about." He went on to say, "There is a song in dancehall they call sey dem a badman a gal a run dem head"

So I say to him, "The great man Marcus Garvey say, 'No real man live without a woman like night to day so a woman to her man'. Even one of the greatest books ever written by man says in it, 'God made Adam and said no man shall be alone so he made Adam a woman and called her Eve'."

He hissed his teeth and said, "I will see you in the club around midnight."

I just looked at him and said, "Ok, my good friend."

I was alone again in this mood that had taken over my whole being. The only thing on my mind was to be a part of someone else's life besides mine. Somewhere deep inside of me I was feeling trapped by a loneliness I just could not put my arms around.

When you give all of yourself to someone or to something, what's left for you?

That's how I was feeling. I was not giving any of me to anyone or anything, but still I couldn't find this happiness I was searching for.

Is life real karma or is it just a selfish world we were brought up in?

Still I was not the kind of man to blame the world for my ways and thinking processes.

***

Anyway, it was getting close to midnight. I took a shower, got ready, and got in my car. On the highway, I saw a car drive past me with a male and a female in the front of the car, and they were smiling so much I almost hit the back of the next car just staring at them.

I pulled over in a gas station to fill my tank. I walked inside the mart at the gas station and saw a couple hugging and kissing and looking so happy. I smiled to myself, paid for the gas and walked out. As I stood pumping my gas, another car pulled up to the pump in front of me. Out of it came another couple.

The man first came out of the car, then the woman. She said, "Love, I am going inside. Do you need anything?"

The man suddenly slapped her on here backside and said, "You got all I want, baby." She laughed and walked off toward the mart in the gas station. The man turned to me and said, "That's a wonderful girl I got there. She is gonna be my wife. She is all a man could ask for." Then he asked me, "Are you married?"

I said, "No. I've never been married."

He said, "I've been married three times. I just never found the right one. Now I met this girl. I know now what was missing from my life. I feel like I was so selfish and I lost everything until the day came and I could see myself living for someone other than me."

My car tank was now filled, so I said, "It was nice meeting you, and thanks a lot for your advice. I wish you all the best."

STEP 5

Overcome temptations

STEP

· Overcome temptations ·

I turned my radio on and this song was on: Me myself and I is all I have in the end. That put me right back in the crazy mood of not wanting to be one with anybody. Now I was in the right vibes for the club.

I drove up and got myself parked and joined the line to get into the club. I could hear a voice calling, "Yow, yow!" As I turned around to look who it was, I felt a hand on my shoulder saying, "We just got here, man. I didn't think you would make it."

I asked, "Why?"

He said, "Because of that fall in love shit you were telling me about."

I said to him, "I get your view. What will happen to us when all we have for ourselves is time, and that's the same thing a woman wants, so how will that work? When I got the kind of cash Jimmy Buffet and Jay-Z have, I will have the time to fall in love."

He replied, "You are still here, man."

I smiled and said, "Let's pay and get in this club and get our party vibes on."

When I got in, though, I felt like the club was like a nightmare. Everywhere I looked there were couples hugging and kissing, dancing to a slow jam, and they were all singing in a loud voice, "I'm so in love with you, anything you ask for I will do."

I was so mad, I turned to my friend and asked him what kind of night it was.

He said, "Ladies night, and it looks like all the ladies brought a male tonight."

This was not the vibes we were looking for. What was going on with all these men nowadays falling in love?

My friend said, "I say we are just late tonight. Let's get something to drink and see in a minute. We will find single ladies in here. It is just the slow jam moment going on."

We walked over to the bar to place our order and there was a beautiful bartender around the counter serving drinks. The first thing I could say to her was, "Wow, good night, beautiful. What are you drinking?"

She smiled and replied, "Nice. I wish I could take you up on that offer but I am married. There's my husband. He is the manager of the club."

I said to myself, "No, this is not happening to me." I couldn't believe it.

I went on and placed the order for me and my friend. We both took a seat at the bar. At that moment we saw a group of five ladies walking into the club.

It was like being in a city on a dark night with no light and suddenly, the lights come on. My friend turned to me and said, "Look there, man, wow."

We started dancing to the music like we were jamming all night cool and humble, like true laid-back thugs. The ladies made their way to the dance floor and started dancing. I kept staring from a distance thinking to myself, what I would not do with one of these ladies tonight. Words can't say. After the next round, my friend said to me, "I am going to get those girls over here."

He left me there still drinking and dancing to the music, building my vibes that I would be going home with one of those girls tonight. I never stopped for a second and thought something bad could happen. I was just thinking of the fun I wanted to have tonight.

I started sipping my drink harder as I could see my friend making his way toward me with the five ladies. They all came over to me and said hello. We exchanged names and I said to them, "What are you ladies drinking?"

One of the ladies replied, "Anything goes." I said, "Wow, you're my kind of girl." We ordered a round and started drinking and dancing. I walked over to one of the ladies and asked for a dance. We started dancing and talking. She asked about my goals in life.

I said, "Become somebody who can hold down my family and give them a good life, like the life I never had." then asked her, "What are yours?"

She said, "To have all you just offered and to have a man who doesn't lie."

I replied, "So, you got a man?"

She said, "Yes I do and he is here."

I say, "For sure?"

She said, "Yes, not to worry, though. He trusts me."

I replied, "If he comes over and sees us dancing, what will he say?"

"Nothing" she said, "He knows I won't do anything out of line with you."

I said to her, "And I am here getting feelings for you, thinking we could get something going from tonight."

She laughed. "I do like your honesty. You will find someone to be all you want one day. Stop looking and let someone find you." Then she said, "Here comes my man."

We stopped dancing and she said, "It was nice meeting you."

It was a true wake-up call for me. Do people really live like this, with this kind of understanding?

Could I be like that?

Could I be in love with someone, sharing my life with them, and we both can do what we want and go wherever we want, without thinking they will be with someone else?

That kind of trust takes strong faith and a heart full of love without strings attached. I needed to truly learn how to love without thinking the person was going to be what you wanted them to be and just love the person for who they are.

I didn't want to be trapped by my way of thinking, though. One of my friends shouted to me, "Are you ok, man? Come over here, come meet my new friends." I went over and made eye contact with a lady.

She was dancing in high heels and wearing a splendid red dress. I said to myself, "Wow, she is stunningly beautiful."

There went my mind again thinking it was just one of those moments of meeting the next beautiful lady and enjoying a night or a few.

Anyway, I had to stop before I went to where my friend was and made the move to introduce myself to the beautiful lady I saw dancing alone.

She beat me to the punch and stepped up to me and said, "Hi, I have been watching you all night."

I told her my name and we hit it off from there. We started

talking like an old fire stick ready to light up again. I forgot my friend was waiting on me. Her smile was like a heavenly light shining.

"You are sweet, boo" She said, "but honestly, I am in no mood to trust so easily. I am going through a bad breakup, so I am just out having fun. Whatever comes, comes. A man will always say the sweetest things to get with you."

STEP

· Have strong faith ·

STEP

· Have strong faith ·

"The amazing, exciting, and breathtaking beauty he craved became the most provoking, overbearing, person on the planet, the one person he can't stand to be around.

I have been faithful for so many years and ended up alone at this age. I am very independent. All I ever ask for is honesty and trust.

I am very open-minded and understanding,

so let's just have a dance and lose ourselves in this moment we got tonight. Who needs tomorrow?"

I replied, "We are all the same kind of people. Beautiful human beings. I believe love must be fun, not painful with tears. Let's drink to that."

"Deep inside," she said, "I know the liquor won't eliminate our fears. It's up to us to overcome with an inner peace and an acceptance of our realities."

Her words were so softly spoken and her story was so touching to my heart. There was no way I could ignore the essence and sentiment of the way her experience had made her feel.

I had arrived at this point in my life because of my experience. I had been in and out of love. From my youthful past, I had learned from my elders. I had read many books written by great minds that have impacted so many people's lives, not only mine. That experience truly is wisdom.

Can a man erase all the things he has learned in the past? Can he change his mindset and open his heart and mind to learn from experience as he grows and lives his one or many lives?

I just could not fight the feelings anymore. The conversation had gotten so intense. My body was so hot and I knew her mouth was moving but her words were so over powering and factual. They no longer were going through my ears. They were cutting through my heart.

She looked right into my eyes as if she was looking deep into my soul. Right then, my knees were about to fail. She reached out and touched me on my shoulder. "Are ok?" She asked.

Looking at her, I replied, "I am ok. But there is just this thing about you. The way you express yourself has taken my mind above the clouds where I can see myself looking down at myself, asking myself if I should be confident or in dismay, or if I should just accept it was meant to be this way."

I thought, "The person you love will always be in love with someone else." This thought has never slipped the grip of my mind for one single day.

Is it love that I am searching for? Or just the excitement of the chase and the unknown?

But why would I be thinking like this now when she is saying all these things I want to hear? Anyway, I'm not looking to be in any commitment right now. Yet my mind keeps wondering more and more.

Boldness and lack of fear sometimes lead to carelessness. In my mind I'm still saying, "What if she is just a sick girl out spreading a virus? Or what if she really is someone single and hurt as she is saying and expressing right now?"

Standing there looking at her, my eyes were all over her body. My mind was far away from all fearful thoughts. It was more on joyful thinking.

She said, "I like something about you. That's why I am here talking to you. I am not trying to bore you down. It's just that the one person I call my friend, is the one person who backstabbed me, broke my heart and stole my love away, so I have no one else to talk to. I don't want to lose my mind, and I just can't be alone. It's killing me softly. That's the only reason I am out here.

I have never done this before. I have never just walked

over to someone and started talking to them like this, but now I am happy I did. It feels like we know each other from some other lifetime before.

You are an amazing listener, not like many other men I have met. You sound like we have both shared the same experience."

After a few more rounds of liquor, she was all up on me and it felt so good. But so bad. I didn't want to feel like I was taking advantage of her vulnerability.

So I said to her, "I know what it is like to be hurt and not thinking right at the moment. So I don't think you know the game you wanna play. You just won't be the same if you don't keep yourself together. Once a good girl gone bad, they gone bad forever."

There is no coming back. Are these just a man's fears? Is it best to use his matureness to hide his tears and not reveal his tender side to show how much he really cares?

These feelings of sorry were not in my blood, veins, or thoughts. Where is this mindset coming from?

I was out clubbing, partying, and my friends were over there having fun. And now I was over here with this beautiful lady feeling sorry for her.

What was I really doing? I should have been trying hard to get her into my place tonight in the comfort of my private settings.

But that was not what I was feeling right then. It was

getting late and the club would soon close, and I was still thinking like a saint, not like a rebel, rude boy, or thug. I was getting an inside feeling of guilt like I was about to do something I was going to regret.

What could I do to overcome this urge? Her body was so sexy. Her lips and her curves and motions and words. How could a man lose a girl like this?

I started to undress her in my mind, imagining all kinds of ways and things I wanted to do to her. I was in my own little world and she was just there standing in front of me smiling.

I was looking at her so strongly and profoundly. She looked into my eyes and said, "Are you ok? It's like your mind is so far away. It can be seen by everyone around us. May I ask what's on your mind?"

Before I could reply, she said, "Have I told you I know how a man thinks? They are more ruled by their pencil than by their heart. A woman is ruled by her heart and emotions, not by her genital parts.

When a woman is hurt, she wants to get over her hurt and rebuild her confidence and fully heal herself before she starts to love again.

I came here tonight to this club to enjoy myself, but I can't stop thinking how my lover broke my heart and left me for my best friend. I just can't be alone right now.

I only have one sister, and she is a doctor and she is always busy at work. She is a single woman, so I don't like dragging her into my relationships. She has her own life. And she always told me, whenever a man is seeking her attention or trying to intrude into her life, she says she is in love already.

But the one man she is in love with from her school days has never said one word to her in school or after, and she has never said one word to him either. So they both went through school never saying one word to each other.

But she really loves that guy. She always says we only get the chance for true love once, just like we only get one mother and one father."

She then held on to one of my hands and asked me, "Are you mad at me? I know I never gave you a chance to answer my question."

I replied, "It's ok. I am learning to be a little more patient and understanding that sometimes a woman just needs someone who can really listen to her without judging her or trying to get her clothes off."

She then said, "Don't be disappointed. You never know what tomorrow brings, and I do love your energy."

So then I told her, "I am here tonight, and I am very grateful to be here alive and well after just experiencing a very bad accident."

She instantly took a deep breath and said, "I am happy you are ok and made it out alive. What kind of accident was it?"

"A car accident on the highway" I replied, "But it's ok. The greatest thing is I am here and I think it made me a changed man. I would not be here talking to you relaxed like this.

Look over there. Those guys are my friends and right now, they would not believe I am over here, having this kind of conversation with you. We came here to find girls tonight to take back to our place to have some fun for the night. But to be truly honest, I am fighting with this thought in my mind.

It takes away my urge for this kind of life at this appointed time in my life. I hear you talking about your sister, and I want to tell you, I went to school with a girl I have been in love with at first sight. The thing is, every time I am around her, I get a weakness in my belly so I never found words or the confidence to tell her I loved her in school.

I never saw her again after school until I had my accident. I was in the hospital and she was the doctor who was assigned to take care of me. I was so shocked. So I finally got the chance to tell her how I was feeling. She has been on my mind every second since coming out of the hospital. She is all I can think about.

I told my friends how I am feeling about her and they said I am losing it and becoming soft. They say when a man has one woman, it makes his penis go dead."

She laughed and said, "You guys are something else. This is what guys talk about when they are together?"

I turned to her and said, "What do ladies talk about when

they are together?"

"That no man can be faithful and loyal to one woman." She replied, then smiled at me and asked, "Can they be faithful to one woman?"

I laughed and said, "What did I start anyway, beautiful lady in red? I am happy to meet you tonight and to have this conversation. It's refreshing. I am truly honored. Your words have helped to open my eyes.

I am confident now that there is no greater binder than energy to bind two people together, on a mental and physical level.

I've learned to love without fear or ego, limit or time. So let's be friends. We might help each other one day. I am going to exit the club now." She hugged me and we both said goodbye for now.

STEP 7

The commitment

STEP

· *The commitment* ·

I turned and walked away from her and went back over to where my friends were hanging out, dancing and drinking,

As I got closer to where they were, they started clapping and then said to me, "Wow. Yes, she is a very beautiful girl. It looks like she will be yours for tonight."

"No sir" I said, "She is not into that kind of conversation and mood right now."

They all started laughing at me, and said, "So what were you over there doing all this time?"

I said, "She is hurt at the moment. She just wanted someone to talk to like a friend, who would just listen sincerely. She said her best friend stole her lover from her, so she trusts no one at this time."

They all started laughing at me again, then asked me, "Are you a babysitter or a marriage counselor?"

As a man, this is how we are at times. Everything is a joke.

I replied, "You can all talk and say what you all want to say. You're the ones here. Make sure you all get what you all are here looking for. I found the girl of my dreams. I want to invest 100% of my time, try to build a foundation and see where life takes us from there."

They laughed at me like it was a joke. "She is really a dream girl that you can only see when you are asleep. But every time you wake up, you never see her, right? You are on a trip!"

I said, "What kind of trip?"

They replied, "From the accident. You are not yourself. We all realized. So get better and we will get back to this topic one day soon. As for right now, we are going to the bar for another round of liquor."

I said, "Okay, drink one for me. Anyway, I am going to make a quick exit from the club. Don't let me spoil the rest of your night. We will all meet up tomorrow on the basketball court."

I walked out of the club, to the car park. My mind started wandering off again.

Thinking of my friends, I said to myself, "To really be a man and to truly be a very happy person requires taking full control of your decision-making without interference from other influences but your deeper and inner feelings."

As I walked towards the car more thoughts were flashing through my mind.

"There is an angel and a demon in all of us.

Let your love be without conditions.

True love must be unconditional, just like nature loves us all."

These thoughts were my final step towards being committed in my mind. So when I am ready physically, there is no more looking away or turning back from love ever again.

**

As the next day broke, I made sure to call the beautiful doctor who has been my school days' crush and invited her out for lunch.

I was so excited when she said yes and accepted my invitation. She said, "I will see you around midday at one of the hot-spots in the city, close to the hospital."

"See you at midday" I replied, "my beautiful wife-to-be."

She said, "Wow, so fast! Anyway, I like your confidence. I got to go back to work now. I will see you in a few hours. Be safe on your journey."

"Thanks, my love." I answered, "I will see you soon."

I had a few errands to run and take care of, so I took a shower and got ready to go on the road. I needed to look like a million bucks today. This was the woman I wanted to make my biggest impression on for the rest of my life, so I didn't want to blow it. I was so nervous. Nothing I found in my closet made me feel confident.

Then I looked into the mirror and talked to myself for a few minutes. The words in my head told me this was a different situation, so I needed a different mindset.

I decided to just put on my jeans and a t-shirt and went out to meet up with my hot date. I had been waiting a lifetime for this moment. I prayed nothing would spoil it or mess it up. I never wanted to hurt this woman I had been dreaming of for so long.

On my way, I pulled over by the shopping mall and bought a bunch of roses and a nice pack of chocolate. It was small, but it was a gift from my heart. It was the thought that counted more than the size and the price of the gift.

I hoped she would truly appreciate this little gift. My heart was pounding so hard. I said in a low voice, "Men will try everything to cover up their emotions."

I hoped she was all the woman I would ever want in this lifetime. And even in my next life.

I arrived at the hot-spot 15 minutes early. She was already there having a drink sitting at a table by a window.

It was a very nice and cozy spot. There was ambient music playing in the background. She was sitting there looking like heaven had opened its door. She was glowing like an angel. Her smile was so innocent like a newborn baby. I walked up to her.

She got up and pulled out one of the chairs from the table, then she walked to meet me before I got to the table. She greeted me with a hug and a kiss on my cheek. Her hug was so tight. It was like she was in the same feeling and frame of mind as I was.

This was my one true love. I felt like I was in space for a minute there in a daydreaming phase.

She said, "Welcome. How was your journey here?"

"Amazing" I said, "Today is the best day of my life."

She smiled. Then I handed her my gift and the roses. She said, "Wow. How sweet of you! It's a pity I did not get the time to get a gift for you. I had it in mind, but don't worry. I will surprise you another time."

I replied, "It's ok, baby. It's from my heart."

She said, "I want to give you one from my heart too. Don't you know the woman who doesn't know how to treat a man, can't keep a man? Likewise, the man who doesn't know how to treat a woman, can't keep a woman."

I replied, "Yes, my baby, that's true. I love the way you talk. Anyway, how was your day, my love?"

She said, "It was productive. I helped save someone's life at the hospital this morning, so that's the best gift I could ask for. Saving lives is the reason I went into the medical field. And now you brought me another gift, and I am also grateful for your presents."

I said, "I am also grateful for your presence here too and for taking this time to talk to me face to face."

"Order yourself a drink" She said, "Let me know what you like. Here is the menu. This is a nice place to relax and dine."

I placed the order for my drink. It was something soft to start off my moment and a glass of water to cool me down until I felt like placing the order for the choicest food that I wanted from off the menu.

She took a sip of the red wine she was drinking, and then said to me, "Let's talk seriously now, about us. What do you really want?

Not just from me, but what does a man really want? What truly makes a man happy inside and outside?

What can a woman do to know and be 100% sure that her man won't go out and cheat on her and take her love for granted and make her waste her time and end up broken-hearted in the end?"

Before I could say one word, she said, "You know, I have been by myself all these years for a reason, because I got no plans to place my trust and give my interest to a man who is like most men who would rather spend most of their time lying than trying to keep their relationship and stay loyal to their commitment.

You will give a person all of you and do any damn thing just to please them and they will be the one to hurt you the most in the end."

I had to say to her, "Hold on one minute, baby. I am not trying to cut your conversation but I can't answer all these questions at once. You started talking like there is a vendetta already out for me, with that expression. Is there one?"

She said, "No-no-no. Baby, don't get it wrong. I am sorry you are taking my words and expressions out of context. That's not the basis of my conversation. It is just to let you know I am a woman who truly believes in being the one and only woman in my man's life, like my man is the only man in my life."

· *The way to the key* ·

· The way to the key ·

So I asked her, "Baby, what makes a woman truly happy? Loyalty? Honesty? Faithfulness?

Confidence in her man both mentally and physically? And to trust his words fully without doubts? Not just trust his words when he his right there beside you or in front of you?

Why is it like that? It doesn't matter how a man trusts his woman. Even if a man just got married to his wife, if you ask her ten minutes after the wedding, if she thinks her husband will cheat on her now that he is married, I am sure she will say yes. I'm not saying all will, but most will."

She laughed out loud and said, "I will answer all your questions in one word, man: 'A dog will have a diamond and cheat with a silver spoon.'"

I said, "Let me tell you, my love, all you need to do to keep a man forever and he will only love you and you alone and never look at or love another woman. He will be fully committed to you, be faithful to you, and never lie to you again, never cheat on you again. He will never give you a doubtful moment to think he is hiding something from you. He will love you unconditionally.

You will always feel like you're the only woman on planet earth."

She said, "Are you sure?"

I said, "Yes I am more sure now than I have ever been. Just let me love you in all the ways you always dreamed of being loved and being treated in both your mental and physical worth.

I see you as the woman you are, deeper than your physical attractions. I see you as inspiring, and influential, and very emotional, still you know how to stay in control mentally, verbally, socially, and at the same time you are so royal in your physical attire."

***

When you want to steal a man's heart, love a man in this way and you will never see a lonely night again. You will never see a reason to fight.

Are you ready to learn the one and only way to truly win a man's heart forever and it will never break apart? Are you ready to truly love a man, and he will never ever hurt you?

It's time to stop asking questions now. Know the answers for yourself.

Printed in Poland
by Amazon Fulfillment
Poland Sp. z o.o., Wrocław

55132512R00045